BOOK 7

More Praise for IVY + BEAN

"Just right for kids moving on from beginning readers . . . illustrations deftly capture the girls' personalities and the tale's humor. . . . Barrows' narrative brims with sprightly dialogue."
—★ *Publishers Weekly*, starred review

"In the tradition of Betsy and Tacy, Ginnie and Genevra, come two new friends, Ivy and Bean. . . . The deliciousness is in the details here. . . . Will make readers giggle."
—★ *Booklist*, starred review

"A charming new series." —*People*

"Ivy and Bean are a terrific buddy combo." —*Chicago Tribune*

"Readers will be snickering in glee over Ivy and Bean's antics."
—*Kirkus Reviews*

"This is a great chapter book for students who have recently crossed the independent reader bridge."
—*School Library Journal*

"Annie Barrows' simple and sassy text will draw in both the reluctant reader and the young bookworm. Fans of Beverly Cleary's Beezus and Ramona will enjoy this cleverly written and illustrated tale of sibling rivalry and unexpected friendship."
—*BookPage*

iVy + BEAN
WHAT'S THE BIG IDEA?

BOOK 7

written by annie barrows + illustrated by sophie blackall

chronicle books · san francisco

For all children's librarians everywhere,
but especially for Mrs. Jean Merian —A. B.

For Leah Brunski, a remarkable teacher —S. B.

Special thanks to Sean Fottrell for information about the science
of global warming.

First paperback edition published in 2011 by Chronicle Books LLC.

ISBN 978-1-4521-0236-8

The Library of Congress has cataloged the hardcover edition as follows:
Barrows, Annie.
Ivy + Bean what's the big idea? / written by Annie Barrows ; illustrated by Sophie Blackall.
p. cm. — (Ivy + Bean ; bk. 7)
Summary: When all the second grade students must enter the science fair, which has global
warming as its theme, best friends Ivy and Bean team up to create an unusual project.
ISBN 978-0-8118-6692-7
[1. Science projects—Fiction. 2. Science fairs—Fiction. 3. Schools—Fiction.] I. Blackall,
Sophie, ill. II. Title. III. Title: Ivy and Bean what's the big idea? IV. Series.
PZ7.B27576Iwbh 2010
[Fic]—dc22
2010008258

Series design by Sara Gillingham.
Book design by Sara Gillingham.
Typeset in Blockhead and Candida.
The illustrations in this book were rendered in Chinese ink.

Manufactured by Leo Paper Products, Heshan, China, in May 2011.

10 9 8 7 6 5 4 3 2 1

This product conforms to CPSIA 2008.

Chronicle Books LLC
680 Second Street, San Francisco, California 94107

www.chroniclekids.com

CONTENTS

BEAN GETS ANTSY

There had been a problem in Bean's house. The problem was staples. Bean loved staples. She loved them so much that she had stapled things that weren't supposed to be stapled. The things looked better stapled, but her mother didn't think so, and now Bean was outside.

She was going to be outside for a long time.

She looked at her backyard. Same old yard, same old trampoline, same old dinky plastic playhouse, same old pile of buckets and ropes and stilts. None of them was any fun. Maybe she could play junkyard crash. Junkyard crash was when you stacked up all the stuff you could find and then drove the toy car into the stack. But it was no fun alone. Bean got up and scuffed across the nice green lawn until she reached the not-so-nice green lawn. This part of Bean's lawn had holes and lumps in it. The lumps were mostly places where Bean had buried treasure for kids of the future.

Bean picked up a shovel. To heck with kids of the future. She was bored *now*. And maybe a secret admirer had added something interesting to her treasure, like a ruby skull or a dinosaur egg.

Bean didn't bury her treasure very deep, so it was easy to dig up. This treasure was inside a paper bag, but the paper bag wasn't doing so well. It wasn't really a paper bag anymore. "Holy moly!" Bean said loudly. "I've found treasure!" She pulled the clumps of paper apart. What a disappointment. No ruby skull. No dinosaur egg. Just the same stuff she had buried two weeks ago: dental floss, tweezers, and a magnifying glass. Some treasure.

Bean flopped over on her stomach. "I'm dying of boredom," she moaned, hoping her mother would hear, "I'm dyyy-ing." She coughed in a dying sort of way, "huh-ACK!" and then lay still. Anyone looking from the porch would think she was dead. And then that person would feel bad.

Bean lay still.

Very still.

She could hear her heart thumping.

She could feel the hairs on her arm moving.

Bean opened her eyes. There was an ant scurrying over her arm. Bean pulled the magnifying glass over and peered at the ant. Her arm was like a mountain, and the little ant was like a mountain climber, stumbling along with a tired expression on his face.

Poor, hardworking ant. She knew how he felt because sometimes her parents made her go hiking. She watched as he dodged between hairs and charged down the other side of her arm toward the ground. She offered him a blade of grass to use as a slide, but that seemed to confuse him. He paused, looked anxiously right and left, and then continued on her arm. He had a plan, and he was going to stick to it. Bean watched through the magnifying glass as he scuttled into the grass, rushing along the ground between blades. He was in a big hurry. He met another ant by banging into him, but they didn't even stop to talk. They zipped off in opposite directions.

Bean followed her ant to a patch of dry dirt. There he plunged down a hole.

"Come back," whispered Bean. She liked her ant. Maybe he would come out if she poked

his house. She found a thin stick and touched the top of the hole. Four ants streamed out and raced in four different directions. Bean didn't think any of them was her ant.

Bean watched the ant hole for a long time. Ants came and went. They all seemed to know where they were going. They all seemed to have important jobs. None of them seemed to notice that they were puny little nothings compared to Bean.

Bean dragged the hose toward the ant hole. She didn't turn the hose on. That would be mean. But she let a little bit of water dribble into the hole, and watched as the dirt erupted with ants. Thousands of ants flung themselves this way and that, racing to safety.

"Help, help," whispered Bean. "Flood!"

The ants ran in lines away from the water. Some were holding little grains above their heads. They were the hero ants. But even the nonhero ants were busy. They were all far too busy to notice Bean watching them through the magnifying glass. To them, she was like a planet. She wasn't part of their world. She was too big and too far away for them to see.

Bean looked up into the sky. What if someone was watching her through a giant magnifying glass and thinking the same thing she was? What if she was as small as an ant compared to that someone? And what if that someone was an ant compared to the next world after that?

Wow.

Bean waved at the sky. Hi out there, she thought.

JUST DESERTS

"Criss-cross applesauce, boys and girls," said Ms. Aruba-Tate.

Along with the rest of the second graders, Bean criss-cross applesauced. Then she sat on her hands for good measure. Rug time was tough. It was the rug. The rug had a map of the United States of America on it. Each day at rug time, all the second graders rushed to sit on Colorado. Colorado was the best state because it had the Rocky Mountains in it. That meant whoever sat on Colorado got to yell "I rock!"

Bean was in Iowa. She didn't rock. She *could* rock. She could lean way over, push Vanessa a tiny little bit, slap the corner of Colorado, and say "I rock!" But then Ms. Aruba-Tate would get mad. Bean knew that from experience. So Bean sat on her hands. Next door, in South Dakota, Ivy was trying to cross one eye without crossing the other. She had been trying all day. She didn't care much about Colorado. Once, she sat on it without even noticing.

Bean decided to pay attention to what Ms. Aruba-Tate was saying. "Today, class, we are having a special science lesson." Science! Bean stopped thinking about Colorado. Science was usually dirt or fish, and Bean liked both of them. But now, Ms. Aruba-Tate went on, "A team of scientists from the fifth grade will be presenting a report on global warming. And what do I expect from you, class?"

"Respectful listening," everyone answered. Almost everyone. MacAdam was pulling nubbies out of the rug, and he didn't say anything.

Bean said it, but she felt only a little bit respectful inside. Nobody listened respectfully to second graders. It wasn't fair.

"Let's welcome our fifth-grade scientists!" called out Ms. Aruba-Tate. The door to the classroom opened and four students shuffled in.

Their names were Juan, Matt, Adrian, and Shayna. Only Shayna talked. Juan, Matt, and Adrian held the posters.

Shayna tossed her hair over her shoulders. "This is a report on global warming," she said. "Adrian, show the desert. This is a picture of the Gobi Desert, but pretty soon almost everywhere is going to look like this because of global warming. Juan, show the polar bear." Juan held up a picture of a worried-looking polar bear. "Now!" Shayna said loudly, "Global warming is a total disaster and it's all our fault."

On the rug, the second graders looked at one another. This did not sound good.

+ + + + + +

When school was over, Ivy and Bean slumped like two sacks of potatoes on the bench outside their classroom.

"Whatcha doing?" asked Leo.

Ivy and Bean looked up. "We're worrying about the polar bears," said Ivy glumly.

"What polar bears?" asked Leo. Leo was in a different class.

"There's not enough ice for them to live on," said Ivy.

"They're going to die out, like the dinosaurs," said Bean.

"The heat's going to get them," said Ivy.

Leo kicked their bench. "You guys want to play stomp tag?"

Ivy and Bean stared at him. "It's the pollution," said Bean.

"From cars," said Ivy.

"And cow poop," Bean
reminded her.

Leo made a snorty sound. He thought cow poop was funny. Ivy and Bean frowned at him. "I'll be it," he said.

"What?" said Bean.

"I'll be it. You can even stomp me for free if you want," said Leo. He stuck his foot out. "Go ahead."

Bean shook her head. "We're busy," she said.

Leo looked up and down the breezeway. It was empty. "What are you busy doing?"

"We're busy worrying," said Bean.

After a while, Leo found some other kids who wanted to play stomp tag, and Ivy and Bean got up and began to worry their way home.

"Poor trees," said Ivy, patting one.

"Yeah," said Bean. She kicked a car parked at the curb. "Take that!" she yelled and felt a little better.

At home, Bean's mom had heard about global warming and even about the polar bears. Bean's dad knew about it, too. Bean's older sister, Nancy, said, "Ha! That's nothing. Just wait until you find out about the oceans."

"What about the oceans?" asked Bean quickly.

"That's for me to know and you to find out," said Nancy. "But it's terrible," she added.

Bean was too worried even to throw something at her. She went into the backyard and wandered across the lawn. Poor grass. Poor trees. She squatted down by the patch of dirt where the ants lived and patted it. Poor ants.

She hated global warming.

HOT AND BOTHERED

The next day, no one rushed to sit on Colorado. Dusit sat in the middle of the Atlantic Ocean without pretending he was drowning. Bean and Ivy flopped onto Wisconsin together.

Ms. Aruba-Tate was explaining capital letters with her big purple pen. The first letter at the beginning of a sentence was always capital.

Okay, thought the second grade.

The first letter of a person's name or a place was always capital, too.

Fine, thought the second grade. Whatever.

Ms. Aruba-Tate put the cap on her big purple pen and looked at the children on the rug. "Well!" she said, "I know something that will pep you up. Emerson School is going to have a science fair!"

"No!" groaned Bean.

"I hate science," said Emma. Drew and Eric nodded.

Ms. Aruba-Tate raised her eyebrows. "I'm confused, boys and girls," she said. "I thought you liked science."

"No. We hate it," Zuzu said. "It's awful."

"But," said Ms. Aruba-Tate, "what about fish prints? You liked making fish prints, didn't you?"

"Those were okay," said Emma.

"And our insect studies," Ms. Aruba-Tate asked. "You liked those, didn't you?"

"That cicada was cool," said Marga-Lee.

"Remember the hissing cock-roach?" said Drew. "That was cool, too."

"What about marine reptiles?" said Ms. Aruba-Tate. "Elasmosaur and plesiosaur?"

"And mosasaur!" yelled Eric. Eric loved mosasaur.

"Then why do you say you hate science?" asked Ms. Aruba-Tate.

"Global warming!" chanted the second graders.

"Global warming?" asked Ms. Aruba-Tate.

"Didn't you listen, Ms. Aruba-Tate?" Bean said. "The whole world is going to turn into a desert."

"The polar bears are going to die out," said Ivy.

"And the frogs," said Emma.

"And newts," said Eric. "Squishy things are in trouble."

"All the animals are in trouble," said Drew.

"And it's all our fault!" said Bean. That was the worst part.

Ms. Aruba-Tate was quiet for a moment. She looked like she was thinking hard. Then she said, "Boys and girls, I'm hearing that you are very worried about global warming. I'm feeling sorry that you're worried, but I'm also feeling glad that you care so much about the earth. People who care as much as you do are the people who will find solutions to the problem."

The second graders looked at each other. Solutions? There were solutions?

"Right now, scientists all over the world are trying to find ways to stop global warming. Science is the solution, not the problem.

That's why I'm sad when I hear you say you hate science."

"They should work harder," said Drew.

Ms. Aruba-Tate looked at him. "Do you remember, Drew, when we talked about cave dwellers? Some of you thought cave dwellers

were stupid, because they didn't know how to build houses, and we talked about how people have to experiment in order to make their lives better. Remember?"

"Yeah," said Emma. "We decided maybe cave men got the idea for houses from watching termites."

"Exactly!" said Ms. Aruba-Tate. "We get ideas, we experiment, and we find solutions to our problems. That's what scientists do."

"But they haven't found the solution to global warming," said Ivy.

"They haven't found one perfect solution, but they've found lots of little ones, like cars that don't pollute so much. Each little solution is a step toward a big solution," said Ms. Aruba-Tate. "Do you think the first house built by a cave man was perfect? No, it probably collapsed—"

"It caved in!" yelled Dusit. Eric and Drew fell over laughing.

"Thank you, Dusit," said Ms. Aruba-Tate. "And the second house probably caved in, too. But each time, the cave dwellers learned something new, and in the end, they built a house that stayed up. They were cave scientists. Scientists don't give up if something doesn't work perfectly; they look for new ideas to make it better." She smiled. "And that reminds me of you. You children have new ideas all the time, which means you're already good scientists. Each one of you could come up with an idea to fight global warming."

"But we're kids," said Vanessa.

"You're kid scientists," said Ms. Aruba-Tate firmly. "What we need for this problem is new ideas. And you kids are great at that."

"Yeah," whispered Bean. She *was* great at new ideas. She had them all the time.

"So—I think we have our theme for the Emerson School Science Fair, don't you?" asked Ms. Aruba-Tate. "Ideas that fight global warming."

Oh, this is going to be great, thought Bean. If she stopped global warming, she'd be the most famous person in the world. "Do you win anything if your idea is the best?" she called out.

Ms. Aruba-Tate smiled. "You sure do. You win a special certificate of Scientific Achievement from the Principal!"

Sheesh. Bean had been hoping for money. But she would fight global warming anyway.

ICEBOUND!

"This would be a lot easier if we had some of those white coats," Bean said. She speared her bagel on her thumb and took a chomp out of it.

"Lab coats," said Ivy, licking her cream cheese. "And lots of little bottles of chemicals."

"What if there was just this one chemical that would stop global warming and we discovered it?" Bean said dreamily. She imagined herself holding up a test tube full

of shimmering pink stuff. TA-DA, she was saying. All around her, other scientists clapped in amazement.

"Don't you remember?" Ivy interrupted her dream. "My mom said she was never going to get me another chemistry set after what happened last time."

"You have some potion ingredients, don't you?" asked Bean. Ivy was going to be a witch when she grew up, so there were usually potion ingredients in her room.

"I've got some dead flies and some baking soda," said Ivy. "And some brick powder."

Bean sighed. "I don't think any of those is going to cure global warming."

"Me neither," said Ivy. "But what will?"

"We have to *think*," said Bean.

Ivy thought and sucked cream cheese out of her hair.

Bean thought and squeezed her head between her hands until her eyeballs almost popped out. "There's recycling, I guess," she

said. "We could show how it's good for the earth."

"But everyone already knows about recycling," said Ivy. "We're supposed to have a *new* idea."

They thought some more.

Bean's dad came into the kitchen. He looked at their thinking faces and sat down at the table next to Bean. "What's happening, kidalunks?"

"We need an idea to stop global warming," said Bean.

"Easy," he said. "Get rid of cars."

"Dad, we're seven. We don't have cars. We need something we can do for a science fair."

"Oh," said her dad. He leaned against the back of his chair and frowned. For several moments it was quiet.

Suddenly, he snapped his fingers. "Okay! Got one! You guys can make posters that remind people to turn out the lights! You

know, to save electricity. You could have a slogan, like 'Lights Out When You're Out!'" He smiled at them proudly. "Isn't that good?"

Bean and Ivy exchanged looks. "Yeah, Dad," said Bean. "Great. Thanks."

"Well!" he said. "I'm going to go clean out the drains."

"Okay," said Bean. Ivy and Bean watched as he left the room. Then they looked at each other and shook their heads. "That has got to be the most boring idea ever," said Bean.

"You know grown-ups," said Ivy. "They don't have very good imaginations."

Ivy and Bean began thinking again.

"What if . . ." began Ivy and stopped. She stared at the refrigerator. "Ice cubes!"

Bean looked at the refrigerator, too. "What about them?"

"Think—how do you cool down a hot thing?" asked Ivy, "Ice cubes! If we could put ice cubes up in the sky, the air would get colder, right?"

"Right," said Bean.

"But how are we going to put ice cubes in the sky?"

"Well, in real life, they'd probably have to drop them out of airplanes, but for the science fair, we could just throw them up in the air to show what we mean."

Bean slapped her hand on the table. "Great idea! And easy, too!"

A minute later, they were running out Bean's back door with all the ice cubes they could find in the freezer. The next minute, they were running back inside to get a thermometer from the bathroom closet. And the minute after that, they both stood on Bean's trampoline, holding bowls full of ice cubes.

"The higher we can throw them, the more they'll cool down the weather," Ivy said, looking at the sky.

"On your mark," said Bean. "Get set. Go!" Together, they began to bounce, higher and higher, higher than they had ever been before.

"I can see my house," yelled Ivy.

"I can see the North Pole!" shouted Bean. But that reminded her of what they were supposed to be doing. "You ready?"

"Yup." Ivy scooped up a handful of ice. "We have to do it quick."

Together, they boinged as high as they could get and hurled the ice up into the air.

"Quick, quick, get the thermometer!" yelled Bean. Flinging her bowl to the ground, Ivy snatched the thermometer and bounced up again, waving it in the air.

"It's definitely cooler up there," said Bean, collapsing onto the trampoline. "What's it say?"

Ivy slowed down and peered at the thermometer. "I don't know," she said. "It looks like 37."

"That's cold," said Bean. "I can feel it. Lookit—I'm shivering." Ivy looked.

Bean's backyard gate swung open. Nancy and her friend Mischa came in, giggling. They stopped when they saw Ivy and Bean. Nancy looked at the lawn. "Why is there ice all over the backyard?" she asked.

Bean would never have told her in a million years, but Ivy didn't have an older sister, so she came right out and answered, "Global warming."

"What?" asked Mischa in a snippy voice. She was Nancy's meanest friend.

"We're curing global warming," said Ivy. "With ice cubes."

Nancy and Mischa burst out laughing. "What*ever*," said Nancy. "Come on, Mischie. But just so you know, guys, ice cubes won't stop global warming. The sun is stronger than a billion ice cubes. And besides, making ice cubes uses up energy. Duh."

"No offense, but that's, like, the dumbest thing I ever heard," sneered Mischa.

Bean looked down at the trampoline. It was covered with melting ice cubes. Quickly, she grabbed up an armful and tossed them at Nancy and Mischa. "Hailstorm!" she yelled. "Watch out!"

At least it was fun to watch them run.

NO MOLD, NO BODY PARTS

Bean and Ivy hadn't found a way to stop global warming, but Bean was willing to bet big money that no one else had either. She was famous for her good ideas and excellent fish prints. Ivy knew more about dinosaurs and prehistoric stuff than anyone in the whole school. If they couldn't figure it out, who could? Take poor Zuzu, for instance. She was going to be an ice skater when she grew up. What did she know about science? Nothing. There was no way she had come up with a good science idea.

But she had.

Zuzu and Emma had decided to plant trees all over the school lawn. In fact, they hadn't just decided it, they had started doing it, during recess. They were digging holes everywhere. "Trees clean the air because they eat car exhaust and make oxygen," said Emma proudly.

Bean had to admit that was pretty good. She and a bunch of kids from Ms. Aruba-Tate's class sat under the play structure and watched Emma and Zuzu dig holes. They had to dig fast so Rose the Yard Duty didn't catch them. Rose the Yard Duty didn't care about global warming.

Eric leaned over the rim of the slide and said, "I'm going to make a garbage robot."

"You mean a robot made out of garbage?" asked Bean.

"How's that going to fix global warming?" asked Ivy. She was reading a paper called "Science Fair Rules."

"It's not a robot made out of garbage; it's a robot that attacks people who litter," Eric said. "I'll hide behind a corner, and when I see some guy drop a cup or something, I'll press the button and this giant robot will come out and crush him.

He'll scream—AAAAHHHH!—but too bad, he's dead."

"Wow," said Bean. It seemed rude to ask Eric how he was going to make the robot.

"Isn't the dead guy kind of like litter?" asked Drew.

Eric disappeared down the slide.

"It says no mold and no body parts," said Ivy, reading.

"Yuck. Mold is gross," said Bean.

"I kind of like it," said Ivy. "But that still doesn't help us think of an idea."

"You guys don't have an idea yet?" asked Vanessa.

"No," said Ivy.

"What's your idea?" asked Bean. Vanessa was either first or best at everything. She even had a retainer already. It was very annoying.

"Okay," began Vanessa, sounding like a teacher, "you know how Shayna said that the earth gets warmer when carbon dioxide gas holds the heat in? Well, guess what? People make carbon dioxide when they breathe out. So, if everyone breathed less, there would be less carbon dioxide, right?" Ivy and Bean nodded. "My idea is I'm going to make all my brothers and sisters hold their breath for fifteen minutes a day. I've got three sisters and two brothers. That's a lot of carbon dioxide." She looked at Bean and Ivy. "Good, huh?"

"No one can hold their breath for fifteen minutes," said Ivy.

"Not all at once," said Vanessa. "A minute at a time, fifteen times in the whole day. I bet I win the certificate."

Bean bet so too, but she didn't say it. She said, "That remains to be seen," in a mysterious voice. But after Vanessa left, she turned to Ivy. "If we don't think of something soon, we're toast."

+ + + + + +

School was over, and Ivy and Bean still didn't have an idea that would stop global warming. They didn't talk much as they walked home. They were thinking.

As they turned the corner of Pancake Court, Ivy and Bean saw Bean's neighbor, Mrs. Trantz, walking her dog Dottsy. Dottsy looked like she was pink, but she wasn't. It was her skin showing through her hair. She and Mrs. Trantz were both old. Whenever they went for a walk, it was a very slow walk.

"Slow down," whispered Bean. "If we catch up to her, she'll get mad at me."

"But you're not doing anything wrong," whispered Ivy.

"I know, but she'll get mad anyhow." Mrs. Trantz was strange that way. You would think she'd get tired of getting mad at Bean, but she never did.

Slowly, slowly, Mrs. Trantz and Dottsy trudged along Pancake Court. Even though she was slower than a slug, Mrs. Trantz acted like she was in a big hurry. Every time Dottsy stopped to sniff a lump of grass, Mrs. Trantz yanked on her leash and said "Come!" in a high voice. Dottsy looked sadly back at each lump as she was dragged away.

"Go slower," whispered Bean.

"I can't go any slower," whispered Ivy. "If I go any slower, I'll be going backwards."

"Let's crawl on our hands and knees," whispered Bean. "We'll pretend we're ants."

They dropped to their hands and knees and crept after Mrs. Trantz, being very slow ants. Little pebbles and sticks dug into Bean's knees, but it was still better than being yelled at by Mrs. Trantz.

"Poor Dottsy," murmured Ivy. "This is all she sees. Rocks and dirt and Mrs. Trantz's behind."

"I'd rather look at rocks than Mrs. Trantz's behind," Bean whispered.

Up ahead, Dottsy turned around and saw them.

"Rrrryp?" she said wonderingly and tried to stop.

But Mrs. Trantz wouldn't let her. She tugged on the leash. "Come!" she snapped.

Dottsy's legs quivered, trying to stay in one place. "Rrryurg," she choked.

Mrs. Trantz turned around to give a really hard yank and saw Ivy and Bean crawling up the sidewalk. "Is that you, Bernice?" she squawked, squinting at Bean.

Bean tried to crawl into some bushes.

"I know it's you! Get up! Stop teasing my dog or I'll call your mother! Get up!"

Bean and Ivy stood up. Ivy bravely said, "We weren't teasing your dog, Mrs. Trantz."

"Who are you, little girl?" yelled Mrs. Trantz. "Leave my poor Dottsy alone!"

"Rrryp?" said Dottsy, sniffing hopefully towards Ivy and Bean.

"Come, Dottsy!" said Mrs. Trantz, giving a giant yank on the leash. Mrs. Trantz was old, but she was strong. Dottsy went flying through the air.

"Poor Dottsy," said Ivy, watching them totter home.

"Yeah," said Bean. "She has a terrible life, and there's nothing she can do about it."

"If I were her, I'd run away," said Ivy.

"But she can't. Mrs. Trantz is bigger than she is. Mrs. Trantz can stick that leash on her and pull her around."

"It's not fair," said Ivy. "People always win."

"Yeah," Bean nodded, watching Mrs. Trantz haul Dottsy up her front steps. "But you know what? Maybe we can make it fair."

SURVIVAL OF THE FITTEST

"Mom," said Ivy, "can you tie this knot?"

Ivy's mom was working in her office. Click, click, click, her fingers jumped along her keyboard. "Mmm," she said.

"Mom?" Ivy said.

"What?"

"Can you tie this knot?"

"Yes," said Ivy's mom. Quickly, she leaned over and pulled on the string wrapped around Ivy's wrists. She tied the ends in a knot.

"Thanks," said Ivy. She and Bean turned to leave. "Bye."

"Mmm," said Ivy's mom, her fingers beginning to jump again.

They walked down the hall to the front door. Walking with their hands tied in front of them was weird. It made their stomachs stick out.

"Wait," called Ivy's mom. She poked her head out of her office. "Can I ask why you've tied your hands together?"

"It's a global warming idea," said Ivy.

"Oh," said Ivy's mom. "What do you mean?"

"Well, you know how lots of animals are in trouble

from global warming?" said Ivy. Her mom nodded. "They'd have a better chance if humans weren't so powerful."

"If humans weren't as strong and smart and stuff," added Bean.

"So we tied up our hands, to make it more fair," said Ivy.

"We thought about hitting ourselves on the head, so that we'd be dumber," said Bean.

"But then we thought that would hurt," Ivy said. "So we picked hands instead."

"If we can't move our hands, we'll be weaker," said Bean. "And then the animals can take over."

"They could take over the world from the people," said Ivy.

"It's a very interesting idea," said Ivy's mom. She smiled. "Where are you going now?"

"We're going to go outside and let the animals see that we're weak," said Ivy.

"We may be eaten," said Bean, "but we don't mind."

"It's for science," said Ivy.

"That's definitely a good cause," said Ivy's mom.

She didn't seem very worried, so Ivy said, "If we do get eaten, bring our skeletons to the science fair."

"Will do," said Ivy's mom and went back inside her office.

+ + + + + +

They stood in Ivy's front yard, trying to show the animals that they were weak.

"Come and get us!" called Bean.

But the animals must have been napping, because it was Katy from down the block who answered. She stepped out of a camellia bush and stared at them.

"What are you doing?" she asked.

"Global warming," said Bean.

"We're fighting it," said Ivy. "We're giving the animals a chance to—"

Katy interrupted. "You want to play Bad Orphanage?"

Katy had changed a lot. When she was little, she had only wanted to play House.

"No, thanks," said Ivy, "We're working on a science project—"

"Just wait right here," said Katy. She crawled into the camellia bush and backed out with a jump rope. "I'm the mean orphanage matron and you're the orphans," she said.

"No," said Ivy again. "We're doing a science project!"

Bean didn't say anything. She loved Bad Orphanage. She loved being the cruel matron who fed crusts to the orphans.

But Katy had her own plan. Katy was stringing her jump rope through their tied hands. "You're my orphan prisoners!" she said and cackled a cruel orphanage matron cackle. "Cry and scream," she ordered them in her normal voice.

"Now wait just a cotton-picking minute here," began Bean. If she didn't get to be a cruel matron, she didn't want to play.

"This is a science project!" yelled Ivy.

Katy paid no attention to them. One thing about Katy hadn't changed. She had always been a tough cookie. "March!" she bellowed, and pulled on her end of the rope.

"No!" said Ivy.

"March or I'll cook you alive!" shrieked Katy. She yanked on the rope again, and Ivy and Bean almost fell over.

Across the street, Sophie W. came out on her porch and saw Ivy and Bean's tied hands. "Whatcha doing?" she called.

"These are my orphan prisoners!" hollered Katy. "Come on! You can be the other cruel matron."

"You're stopping scientific progress!" Ivy yelled.

"Right!" yelled Bean. "This is about global warming!"

"Wrong!" yelled Katy. "This is about orphans!"

Sophie W. ran around Pancake Court, and joined Katy dragging them along the sidewalk. Ivy and Bean twisted and turned their hands, but they couldn't undo the knots in the rope.

"Now let's dump them in the orphanage basement," Sophie said. She pointed at Katy's front yard. "That's the orphanage basement."

"And then let's give them the rack," suggested Katy.

"HEY!" yelled Ivy and Bean together.

"Oh, don't worry," said Sophie. "We won't hurt you for real."

Katy cackled. She might hurt them for real.

She tied them tightly to her porch railing. "Let's get another rope," she said. "So we can stretch them."

"Yeah!" said Sophie W.

Together, they ran off, laughing.

"Boy," said Bean. "That Katy is a wacko. Let's get out of here."

They wiggled their hands, trying to loosen the ropes. It was too bad that Ivy's mom tied knots so well.

"You know," said Ivy. "This is exactly what Dottsy must feel like."

Bean looked at the rope that connected them to the railing. "Isn't this what we were trying for? We're weak and we can't do anything."

Ivy nodded.

"I don't think this is making the animals stronger," Bean said.

"No. I guess it's not," said Ivy.

Bean shook her head. "Bummer. I thought we were on to something."

"Me too," said Ivy. "It might work if all the people in the whole world tied their hands together."

"Especially Katy," said Bean. "But I guess making people weaker won't make animals stronger, unless the animals know it."

"Now we have to think of another idea," sighed Ivy.

They heard the slap-slap of Katy's sandals as she zoomed along the sidewalk. "We have *two* ropes and we're going to string you up!" she yelled. "Prepare to meet your maker!"

RICE AND BEAN

MacAdam had made a battery out of a lime, a penny, and a paper clip. He showed it to the class and then he showed a picture of a car with a zillion limes attached to it. The limes made the car go.

"So MacAdam's idea is to use limes instead of gasoline to fuel cars. Is that it, MacAdam?" said Ms. Aruba-Tate.

MacAdam nodded.

"Very good idea, MacAdam," said Ms. Aruba-Tate. "Limes are a clean kind of energy, aren't they? Clean energy means energy that doesn't make pollution. Scientists all over the world are trying to find clean energy to use instead of gasoline. Can anyone think of another kind of clean energy?"

Bean and Ivy exchanged looks. How come they hadn't thought of limes? How come MacAdam had? "Must be something in the dirt," whispered Bean. MacAdam liked to eat dirt.

"Yes, Bean? Can you think of another kind of clean energy?" Ms. Aruba-Tate said eagerly.

What? Clean energy? She should know this! Bean panicked. "Rice!" she yelled.

"Rice?" Ms. Aruba-Tate looked surprised and interested. "Wow! Is that what your science fair project is about?"

Bean didn't know what to say. "Yes!" she yelled. "Rice energy! It's clean!" She couldn't stop yelling. Ivy was looking at her like she'd lost her mind. "Ivy and I have discovered rice energy!"

"That's great, girls," said Ms. Aruba-Tate. "I'll be excited to see that."

"Me too," muttered Ivy.

RICE!

+ + + + + +

That afternoon at Bean's house, Ivy was the lookout. That meant she stood outside the kitchen door, watching for Bean's mom. If Bean's mom came along, Ivy was supposed to fall on the floor and screech.

Inside the kitchen, Bean was standing on the counter. She was looking through the cupboards, trying to find rice. No luck. She wished she had said she was going to make chocolate chip energy. She knew where the chocolate chips were.

Crackers, more crackers, walnuts, ugly dried lumps she had never seen before, oatmeal . . . rice! Bean grabbed a handful and stuffed the package back on the shelf. "Got it!" she whisper-shouted to Ivy.

Ivy zipped into the kitchen. Bean jumped to the floor and held out her hand. There it was.

A bunch of rice. There was no way they were going to get a Certificate of Scientific Achievement for rice. If only she had kept her mouth shut. "What the heck are we going to do with this?" she said.

Ivy looked at the grains, and her eyes got narrow. "There was this lady," she began.

"Who?" Bean interrupted.

"Lisa Something," said Ivy. "She was a scientist. I read about her in my *Famous Women of Science* book. She said you could get energy by breaking stuff into bits."

"Cool!" said Bean. "Why don't we just break some glasses, then?"

Ivy frowned. "Not those kind of bits. Tiny bits. In the book, she said atoms, which are really tiny bits, but I bet it would work with rice, too. She said there was lots of energy inside tiny things, once you broke them."

It was a weird idea. When Bean broke stuff, it just lay there, broken. It didn't start jumping around energetically.

Bean looked at the rice in her hand. It didn't seem like there could be anything inside rice except more rice, but it was worth a try. "I'll go get some hammers."

GRAND SLAM

Bean thought her mom might not be happy if they hammered rice on the dining room table, so she and Ivy went outside. They found a board in the garage and laid it down on the grass. Bean and Ivy each took a grain of rice and set it on the wood. Then they slammed it with their hammers as hard as they could.

Cool. Rice dust.

They set out two more grains of rice. Slam! More rice dust.

Slam! Slam! *Slam!*

The board leaped up and flipped over, spilling rice dust into the lawn. "Hey! Did you see that board jump?" said Bean. "That's energy for sure!"

"And no pollution," said Ivy. "Let's do it again!"

"It's a science experiment! We *have* to do it again," yelled Bean, lifting her hammer over her head.

"Don't tell me this is another dorky solution for global warming," said Nancy. She and Mischa stood over them in the grass.

"None of your beeswax," said Bean.

"We're making clean energy," Ivy said at the same time. Bean shook her head. Now they were in for it.

"No offense, but you guys are totally lame," giggled Mischa.

Bean could have banged Mischa's toe with the hammer, but she didn't. Ivy was talking. "Don't you care about global warming?" she asked Mischa.

"Bor-ing!" said Mischa. "I'm, like, if I hear about global warming one more time, I'm gonna scream."

"Don't you care about the polar bears?" asked Bean.

Mischa shrugged. "Not really."

"Don't you care about nature?" asked Ivy.

Mischa rolled her eyes. "Bor-*ing*," she said.

"What?" asked Ivy.

"Camping and all that," said Mischa, shaking her head. "Totally boring."

"What *do* you like?" asked Ivy.

"Shopping!" said Mischa.

"And Harky," added Nancy, giggling. Mischa screamed and hit Nancy with her backpack, and they went inside.

Ivy stared after them. "What a couple of weirdos."

Bean dropped her hammer into the grass and went to look at her ant friends in the dirt patch. They were still very busy, zipping to and fro on ant business. They still didn't notice her at all.

"Look," she said to Ivy. Ivy came over and knelt next to her. "Watch these guys. They have no idea that we're here."

Ivy put her finger down in front of an ant. For a moment he stopped, and then, looking annoyed, he climbed over her finger and bustled away.

Ivy and Bean lay on their stomachs, watching the ants. After a while, Ivy said, "I think they know we're here, but they don't like to think about it. We make them nervous."

"Yeah. We're so big."

Ivy was quiet for a moment. "Do you think that Mushie girl is just pretending to hate nature? I mean, how can anyone hate nature?"

"Well," Bean thought. "Maybe she's scared of it. Have you ever been camping and you wake up in the middle of the night and it's more dark than anything in the world and you hear sticks cracking?"

"No," said Ivy. "I've never been camping, but sometimes the same thing happens to me in my own room."

Bean nodded. She knew what that was like. "One time, when we were camping, we thought we saw a bear, and my mom freaked out. She ran to the car and made my dad drive us home, even though we were supposed to stay another night. She couldn't take it. Nature freaks her out."

"My mom is always thinking I'm going to get poison oak and ticks when I go outside," said Ivy.

Bean sighed. "Grown-ups are scaredy-cats."

"They can't help it," said Ivy. "They hate surprises."

A long line of ants made its way past Ivy and Bean. They looked so sure of themselves, but Bean knew that if she dripped water on them, they'd go nuts.

"You know, what really freaks grown-ups out is not being in charge," said Ivy. "Kids are used to not being in charge. That's why we're not scared of nature."

"Grown-ups and ants are a lot alike," Bean said. "If they relaxed a little, they'd have a better time," said Bean.

Ivy rolled over onto her back and looked at the sky. "If grown-ups weren't scared of nature, they'd probably try harder to save it from global warming."

"You're probably right," said Bean. She sat up. "What if we did our science project on teaching grown-ups to be happy in nature? Is that a global warming solution?"

Ivy sat up, too. "Sure it is," she said. "It's definitely fighting global warming because if they loved nature, they wouldn't drive stinky cars."

Bean pictured grown-ups dancing around in a forest, looking happy. "They'd be inspired to save the trees and stuff," said Bean. "None of the other kids have thought of changing grown-ups."

"I bet we get that certificate thing," said Ivy.

"Too bad it's not money," said Bean. "But I don't care, really."

"Maybe we'll get money later," said Ivy.

"Okay, we have to teach grown-ups to like nature," said Bean. "What should we do?"

They thought.

"I guess we shouldn't take them out into the forest and leave them, right?" Bean asked.

"Remember? They don't like surprises. And we don't want to scare them. We want them to be happy," said Ivy.

"Okay, what makes grown-ups happy?" Bean said.

They thought some more.

"They like calm things," said Ivy.

"And quiet things," said Bean. Grown-ups were forever telling her to be quiet.

"And pretty things," said Ivy.

"And they like to rest, too," said Bean. "Grown-ups are always tired."

SCIENTIFIC PRINCIPALS

"Welcome to the Emerson School Science Fair!" said a big sign over the cafeteria door. There was the Principal, standing by the door, saying hello to parents. She was smiling, but Bean thought you could never be too careful about principals. "I know a shortcut," she said to her mom and dad. "Let's go through the kitchen."

Once they were inside, Bean and her parents met up with Ivy and her mom.

"Where's your project, girls?" asked Ivy's mom.

"Our class is over here," said Bean quickly. "Let's go."

Sure enough, there was Ms. Aruba-Tate, next to a table marked "Room Twelve: Global Warming."

Before her parents could start yakking with Ms. Aruba-Tate, Bean dragged them over to a bench where five kids were sitting in a row. "Look," she pointed. "That's Vanessa's project."

Her mom and dad looked. "Looks like a pack of kids to me," her dad said. "What's the project?"

"Wait. You'll see," said Bean.

"Five," yelled Vanessa, holding a small clock. "Four. Three."

"I have to go to the bathroom," said one of the kids.

"No you don't. Two. One. Go!" All together, the five kids took a deep breath and held it.

"These are my brothers and sisters," Vanessa explained to the watching parents. "We're reducing carbon dioxide by not breathing out. Toby can hold his breath for seventy-six seconds. If everyone stopped breathing out for fifteen minutes a day, the world would be a lot cooler." She looked at her clock again. "Five. Four. Three. Two. One."

"Whew." The kids blew out their held-up breaths. Their faces were red.

"Are you guys doing yours soon?" Vanessa called to Ivy.

Ivy made a shh-face and turned to her mom. "Come on, Mom. I want to show you MacAdam's lime car."

MacAdam was hiding under the table, but he had a real lime with a paper clip and a penny in it and his drawing on the top of the table. It smelled good. Next door was

Eric's project. He hadn't had time to build the garbage robot, so he had used one of his toy robots to show his idea. A little plastic man had just tossed a clump of paper on the ground. He was smiling. He had no idea that behind him, a robot was glaring, waiting to whack him on the head. Eric had also made a poster. It read, "Clean Up or Else!"

Next to Eric's robot was a vacuum cleaner. Dusit's idea was to vacuum up all the heat, put it in a giant bag, and send it into outer space. In real life, it would have to be a special vacuum cleaner, but he had brought in a regular

one as an example. "So that's where it went,"
his mom said.

Marga-Lee had made a picture of Earth
with mirrors sticking up all over it. She said
that the mirrors would reflect the sun's rays
back out into space.

"Wow," said Bean's dad, looking at her
picture. "Pretty good idea."

Bean almost said "Wait 'til you see ours,"
but she didn't. She looked at Ivy and made
a mouth-zipping sign. Ivy nodded.

Drew had made a baking soda
and vinegar volcano. It didn't
have much to do with global
warming, but it was fun to
watch the foam spurt out
of the top. He had put
green food coloring in
the vinegar.

Emma and Zuzu had taken about two hundred pictures of themselves digging holes and planting trees. There was also a picture of Rose the Yard Duty yelling at them for digging holes in the school lawn. Underneath, Emma had written "Doesn't care about global warming."

"But Ivy," said Ivy's mom, "where's your project?"

Ivy gave Bean a help-me look, but then, just in the nick of time, Ms. Aruba-Tate interrupted. "Excuse me, may I borrow your daughters?" she asked. "It's almost time," she said to Ivy and Bean.

"We have to go do our project," explained Bean to her parents.

"But what *is* it?" asked her mom.

"It's a secret," said Ms. Aruba-Tate. "You're going to find out in a few minutes. Right, girls?"

"Right," they agreed.

Grown-ups don't usually do what kids tell them to do, so Bean and Ivy had asked Ms. Aruba-Tate to give the orders.

Ms. Aruba-Tate spoke into a microphone. "All available parents, please come to the back of the cafeteria. Come to the back of the cafeteria." She had to say it twelve times before the parents obeyed.

"And they get mad at us if they have to say things twice," whispered Bean to Ivy.

Finally, a group of grown-ups was clustered at the back of the cafeteria.

"Okay," said Ms. Aruba-Tate. "This is Bean." She pointed to Bean. "And this is Ivy."

She pointed to Ivy. "Follow them. The other teachers and I will stay with the kids."

"Is this your project?" asked Bean's dad.

"Yes," said Bean. "Come on. Follow us."

"Where are we going?" asked someone's mom.

"Just outside," said Ivy. "Not far. Come on."

"How long is this going to take?" asked another mom.

"Not long. Don't worry," said Bean.

With grown-ups crowded behind them, they walked across the cafeteria and out the door into the cool night air. The grown-ups

were mumbling things like "What's going on?" and "It's late" and "Sorry!" when they bumped into each other. But since a teacher had told them to, they all followed Ivy and Bean across the playground to the lawn. The light from the cafeteria was very dim. You could just barely see that the lawn was covered with rugs and blankets.

Ivy and Bean stopped and the grown-ups bunched up around them. "Here's what's going to happen," said Bean. "There's a blanket or rug or yoga mat for each of you. We'll take you out with our flashlights and show you a good spot. Then you just lie down."

"And then what?" asked Ivy's mom. She sounded worried.

"And then you rest," said Ivy. "Don't be nervous," she added to her mom. "I'll be right here."

"What does this have to do with global warming?" asked Dusit's mom.

Ivy smiled mysteriously, but no one could see her in the dark. "Just try it," she said.

Ivy and Bean showed all the grown-ups where to lie down. It was lucky that Ms. Aruba-Tate had brought extra towels, because there were more grown-ups than they had planned for. Even the Principal wanted to lie down. Bean gave her an entire blanket all to herself.

Soon there were grown-ups scattered all across the grass. In the dark, they looked like laundry.

"Now," said Bean in a loud voice. "Look up into the sky. Smell how nice the grass is. Listen to the trees. And just rest. Don't talk. Don't do anything. And don't worry. You're totally safe."

HAPPY ENDING

A few grown-ups muttered. Bean heard someone say something about bedtime. One dad sat up, but he flopped down again when he saw Bean coming toward him.

In a minute or two, the grown-ups got quiet. Ivy and Bean heard some gentle sighs. Ivy poked Bean in the ribs. "See," she whispered. "They're getting happy."

Bean was getting happy, too. She couldn't lie down, because she was taking care of the grown-ups, but she could feel the cool night air and she could listen to the leaves move. She could smell the damp dirt under the grass.

She and Ivy stood side by side, making sure that nothing surprising happened. "I think they're liking nature," whispered Ivy.

"I think so, too," whispered Bean. For just a moment, she felt like the grown-ups were the little ants and she was the giant who understood how big the world really was.

A grown-up began to snore softly. Way out on the lawn, the Principal curled up on her side.

Ivy checked Ms. Aruba-Tate's glow-in-the-dark watch. "Two more minutes," she whispered.

Ivy and Bean watched the grown-ups resting. The two minutes passed.

"All right, grown-ups," said Ivy gently. "It's time to get up now."

Some of the grown-ups moaned a tiny bit. They didn't want to get up. Eventually, they struggled to their feet. Except for three who had fallen asleep. Bean woke them up nicely. It would have been fun to pour water on their faces, but that wouldn't have made them happy.

When all of them were on their feet, Bean said, "Okay. That was our science project. You can go now."

But they didn't. They stood looking at her and Ivy.

"Wait," said a mom. "How was that about global warming?"

Ivy and Bean glanced at each other. Even in the dim light, Bean could see that the grown-ups were confused. "Were you happy?" asked Bean.

"What?" said the mom.

"Were you happy while you were lying down?" asked Bean.

"Well, yes," said the mom. "Sure. It was great."

"That's it," said Ivy. "We wanted you all to feel happy in nature."

"So you would care about global warming," explained Bean.

There was a little pause. Bean and Ivy looked at each other—what was so hard to understand?—and then the mom said, "Oh. I get it."

The other grown-ups smiled. "That's a good one," said a dad. "That's a really good one." The other grown-ups yawned and nodded. They began to drift back to the cafeteria, except for Ivy and Bean's parents.

Ivy's mom took Ivy's hand. "I was happy," she said.

"Really? You weren't worried about poison oak and bugs?" Ivy asked.

"At first, I was, a little bit. But then I did what you said, Bean, and smelled the grass and listened to the trees. I haven't done that in a long time."

"And now you care about global warming?" Ivy asked.

"Sure I do."

Ivy turned to Bean. "It worked!"

Bean elbowed Ivy. "Of course it worked. It couldn't help working. It's science."

As they walked back to the cafeteria to give Ms. Aruba-Tate her watch, Bean's dad put his arm around her shoulder. "That was a great science project, sweetie. Much better than my poster idea."

Bean gave him a squeeze. "Oh, Dad, don't feel bad. You're a grown-up. You can't help it."

Ivy and Bean let the grown-ups walk ahead. "They're all caring about global warming now," said Ivy. "I can tell."

"We should give classes," said Bean.

"It would have been nice if we had found the one big solution to global warming," said Ivy.

"Yeah," said Bean. "But we had lots of good small ideas."

"And we're only beginners," said Ivy. "If the two of us work on global warming for ten more years, I bet we find the solution."

Once again, Bean pictured herself holding up a test tube full of shimmering pink stuff while white-coated scientists gasped in amazement. "The first thing we need to do," said Bean, "is to get our hands on a really dangerous chemistry set."

The End.

WHY CAN'T WE JUST THROW ICE CUBES IN THE AIR?
And Other Ideas about Global Warming

What is global warming, anyway?

Everyone likes to be cozy and warm, but too warm is bad. Too warm is sweaty and gross. You all know that people and cars and factories have put a lot of pollution in the air. There's a thick layer of pollution way up in the sky. It isn't so thick that the sun's warmth can't get down to the earth, but it is so thick that the heat can't bounce off the earth and return to outer space where it started. That's what's supposed to happen, but it can't. The heat is trapped down here, in our atmosphere (otherwise known as the sky surrounding our planet). Because of this, the planet is getting hotter and hotter. People may not notice it while they're walking around, going to school, playing soccer, and eating breakfast, but it's happening.

You would really notice it if you were in the North Pole, where the ice is melting, which is bad news for creatures that live on the ice, like polar bears. You would also notice it if you were a frog who wanted to live in a stream that had dried up, or a bird who wanted to build a nest in a redwood tree that couldn't grow without plenty of nice cold fog.

Global warming is bad for animals and plants, for sure. It's also bad for us, because really, who wants to live in a world without frogs? Not me. And even if you think you could manage to live without frogs, you have to think about what frogs do. Among other things, they eat mosquitoes. So, no frogs equals many more mosquitoes. Scratch, scratch, scratch. And that's just one example.

So how can this problem be fixed? Some people are trying to figure out ways to let the heat out of our atmosphere.

Some are trying to clean up the pollution that's floating around up there. Some are trying to make cars and factories that pollute less in the first place. It's hard, though. It's hard because almost every solution involves people giving something up. Take recycling, for instance. Recycling is good for the earth because if you can reuse stuff, it doesn't have to be made all over again, which means less factory pollution. Cool. But recycling also means you have to get up off your duff and find the right recycling bin, and sometimes you have pick your old disgusting hot dog wrapper out of the garbage can and put it in the recycling bin. Still, in comparison to no polar bears or frogs, it doesn't seem like much to complain about.

But recycling is just one tiny example of a solution. What are some others?

Let's look at some of the ideas Ms. Aruba-Tate's students had.

1. Why can't we just throw ice cubes in the air? As much as I hate to admit it, Nancy is right about this one. The sun is stronger than all the ice cubes we could make on Earth AND the energy it takes to make all those ice cubes causes pollution. Darn.

2. Why can't we plant a whole bunch of trees that will eat up all the pollution? We can and we are. Areas where trees got chopped down a hundred years ago are being replanted with new trees. The problem is that we can't plant enough trees to eat up all the pollution because we don't have enough space.

3. Why can't everyone stop breathing so much? It's true that people breathe out carbon dioxide, which is one of the gases that's holding the heat in our atmosphere. But breathing makes so little carbon dioxide compared to, say, driving a car, that holding your breath won't make that much difference. It's probably not good for you, either.

4. Why can't cars run on limes instead of gasoline? They can, but it would take so many limes that we'd have to rip out all the trees we've got and replace them with lime trees in order to get enough to fuel just a couple hundred cars. What we need is "clean energy," which means fuel that doesn't pollute, and is easy to find or make. There's got to be a great clean fuel out there somewhere. It's probably something that's lying around all over the place, something no one has realized could be used for fuel. What could it be? Earwax?

5. Why can't we get energy by breaking stuff into bits? We can.
It's called nuclear fission, and the person who thought of it was Lise Meitner (Ivy calls her "Lisa Something"). The stuff you break has to be tinier than rice, though. You have to break the centers of atoms, which are almost the tiniest things on the planet, but very strong. When you pull them apart, they release a whole lot of energy. This is great, because energy is what we need, except that breaking them apart requires an enormous machine that's really expensive. Also, it causes a lot of another kind of pollution that's dangerous to plants and animals.

6. Why can't we vacuum up all the heat and send it out into space? Scientists are working to make artificial trees that suck carbon dioxide out of the air, which is kind of like a vacuum cleaner. A real vacuum cleaner–type machine wouldn't work because the heat is inside the earth and the oceans, and how is a vacuum cleaner going to slurp heat out of an ocean? Also, because rockets use lots of fuel, the amount of heat caused by sending the vacuum cleaner bag into space would add back all the heat you had just subtracted.

7. Why can't we put up mirrors to reflect the sun's rays back before they get trapped under our pollution? It's a good idea, and scientists are working on it. Some scientists are thinking about putting giant mirrors in the desert, but that would be really expensive because the mirrors would have to be enormous. Some are thinking about putting a bunch of tiny mirrors in outer space, but there's that blasting-off problem again.

SO WHAT CAN WE DO?

There is probably not one thing that will fix global warming (unless I'm right about earwax), but if everyone works at it to the best of his or her ability, we might be able to have a world we all want to live in.